BARBARA REID

Sing a Song of
BEDTIME

North Winds Press
An Imprint of Scholastic Canada Ltd.

The illustrations for this book were made with Plasticine,
shaped and pressed onto illustration board.

The text type was set in 24 point Esprit Book

Photography by Ian Crysler.

Library and Archives Canada Cataloguing in Publication

Reid, Barbara, 1957-, compiler, illustrator
Sing a song of bedtime / Barbara Reid.

ISBN 978-1-4431-4684-5 (bound)

1. Nursery rhymes. 2. Bedtime--Juvenile poetry.
I. Title.

PZ8.3.R29Si 2015   j398.8   C2015-904616-5

www.scholastic.ca

6 5 4 3 2 1   Printed in Canada 114   15 16 17 18 19

MIX
Paper from
responsible sources
FSC® C016245

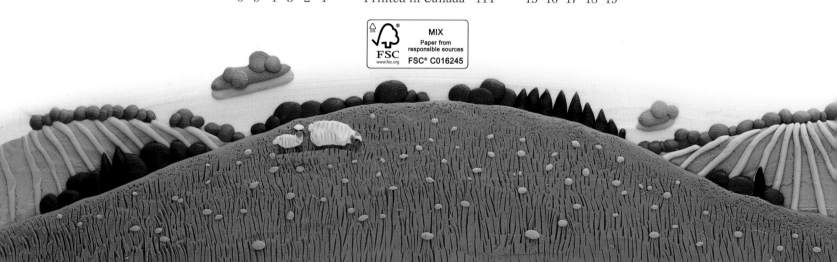

To Peachy and Albert
— *B.R.*

Are You Sleeping/Frère Jacques

Are you sleeping, are you sleeping,
Brother John, Brother John?
Morning bells are ringing,
Morning bells are ringing,
Ding, ding, dong! Ding, ding, dong!

Frère Jacques, Frère Jacques,
Dormez-vous? Dormez-vous?
Sonnez les matines, sonnez les matines,
Ding, ding, dong! Ding, ding, dong!

Little Boy Blue

Little Boy Blue,
Come blow your horn,
The sheep's in the meadow,
The cow's in the corn;
Where is that boy
Who looks after the sheep?
Under the haystack,
Fast asleep.
Will you wake him?
No, not I,
For if I do,
He's sure to cry.

Row, Row, Row Your Boat

Row, row, row your boat,
Gently down the stream.
Merrily, merrily, merrily, merrily,
Life is but a dream.

Sleep, Baby, Sleep

Sleep, baby, sleep,
Your father tends the sheep;
Your mother shakes the dreamland tree,
And from it fall sweet dreams for thee;
Sleep, baby, sleep,
Sleep, baby, sleep.

Sleep, baby, sleep,
Our cottage vale is deep;
The little lamb is on the green,
With snowy fleece so soft and clean;
Sleep, baby, sleep,
Sleep, baby, sleep.

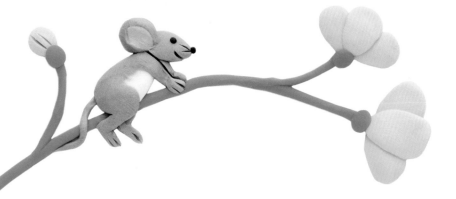

There Was an Old Woman
Who Lived in a Shoe

There was an old woman who lived in a shoe;
She had so many children
She didn't know what to do.
She gave them some broth without any bread,
Then kissed them all soundly
And put them to bed.

Diddle, Diddle, Dumpling, My Son John

Diddle, diddle, dumpling, my son John,
Went to bed with his trousers on;
One shoe off, and one shoe on,
Diddle, diddle, dumpling, my son John.

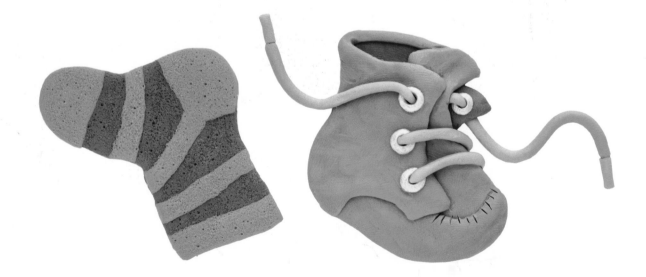

Wee Willie Winkie

Wee Willie Winkie runs through the town,
Upstairs and downstairs in his nightgown,
Tapping at the window,
Crying through the lock,
"Are the children all in bed?
For now it's eight o'clock."

Jack Be Nimble

Jack be nimble,
Jack be quick,
Jack jump over
The candlestick.

The Man in the Moon

The man in the moon
Looked out of the moon,
And this is what he said:
" 'Tis time that, now I'm getting up,
All children are in bed."

Star Light, Star Bright

Star light, star bright,
First star I see tonight;
I wish I may, I wish I might,
Have the wish I wish tonight.

A Wise Old Owl

A wise old owl lived in an oak,
The more he saw, the less he spoke.
The less he spoke, the more he heard;
Why can't we all be
Like that wise old bird?

Teddy Bear, Teddy Bear

Teddy bear, teddy bear, turn around,
Teddy bear, teddy bear, touch the ground,
Teddy bear, teddy bear, reach up high,
Teddy bear, teddy bear, touch the sky,
Teddy bear, teddy bear, bend down low,
Teddy bear, teddy bear, touch your toes,
Teddy bear, teddy bear, go to bed,
Teddy bear, teddy bear, rest your head,
Teddy bear, teddy bear, turn out the lights,
Teddy bear, teddy bear, say "good night."

Hush, Little Baby

Hush, little baby, don't say a word,
Mama's gonna buy you a mockingbird.
And if that mockingbird won't sing,
Papa's gonna buy you a diamond ring.

And if that diamond ring turns brass,
Mama's gonna buy you a looking glass.
And if that looking glass gets broke,
Papa's gonna buy you a billy goat.

And if that billy goat won't pull,
Mama's gonna buy you a cart and bull.
And if that cart and bull turn over,
Papa's gonna buy you a dog named Rover.

And if that dog named Rover won't bark,
Mama's gonna buy you a horse and cart.
And if that horse and cart fall down,
You'll still be the sweetest little baby in town.

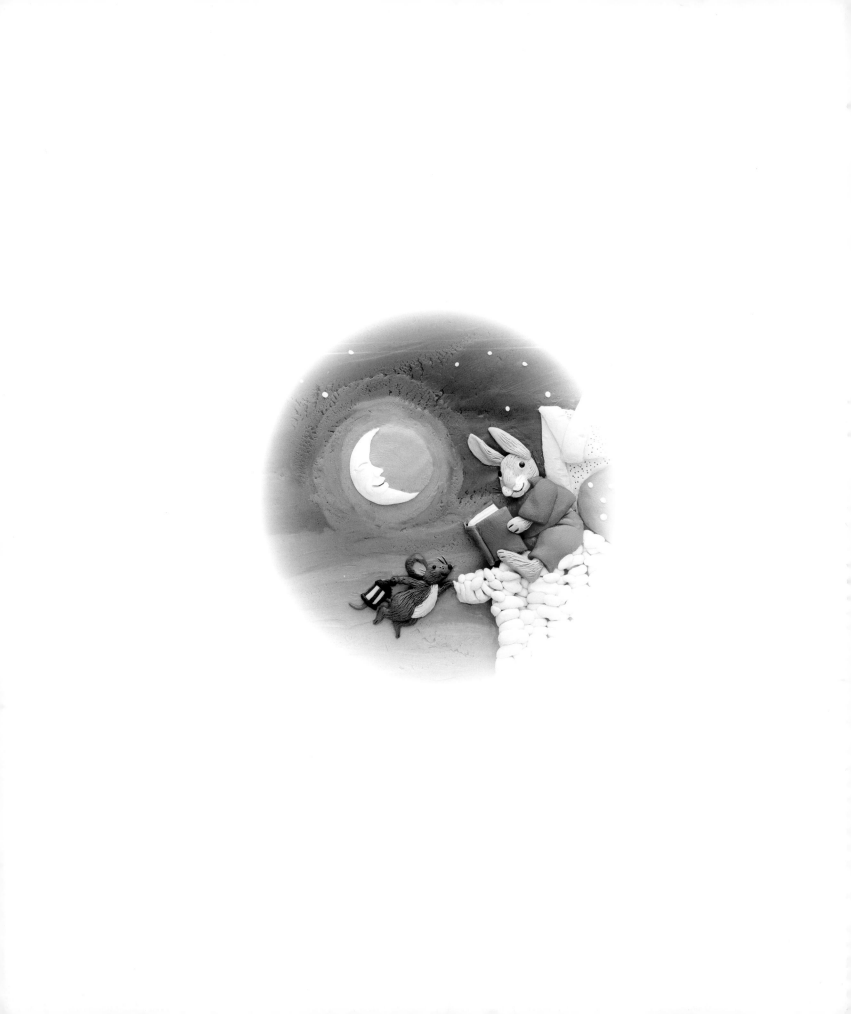